London Borough of Tower Hamlets

910000008093680

D1465609

LoVe MonsteR
& the Extremely Big WaVe

Rachel Bright

HarperCollins *Children's Books*

The sun was up and so was this monster.

(Hello, Love Monster.)

He was going on a VERY
exciting adventure
to the beach ...

...with his friends!

Love Monster couldn't wait!

He just KNEW he was
going to be . . .

From the top of the beach,
the waves looked tiny.

"Ooooo!"
thought Love Monster,
"Surfing is going to be
sooOOOOoo easy!"

But, as they got closer, somehow
the tiny waves began to look,
well . . .

...a tiny bit

BIGGER.

But, it seemed only one monster had noticed the extreme bigness of the waves, and quicker than you can say, "Race you there!"...

everyone was in the water.

Well ...

almost everyone.

Love Monster decided
it was probably sensible
to stay on dry land
for a bit...

You know...

to prepare.

So he did a few
star jumps.

And tried to
touch his toes...

...all the while looking at the extremely big waves and his friends enjoying them.

"Come on in, Love Monster! This is SO. MUCH. FUN!"

Suddenly, Love Monster wasn't
sure he WAS going to be
THE. BEST. SURFER.
IN. THE. WORLD.

In fact, he was wondering if he would
be able to do it at all.

But, after a bit more stretching and a LOT more thinking, there was nothing else to do but dip one toe in the ocean . . .

then another.

And, as a little wave rolled over his feet,

Love Monster thought, "Ha! This isn't so bad."

But then . . .

ASH!

Oh dear, poor
Love Monster.

He was quite sure that what he had just done
was pretty much the opposite of being

THE. BEST. SURFER.
IN. THE. WORLD.

And now, he was right back where he started.

Or was he?

"WooOOHoOOOo!"

"Well done,
Love Monster!"
His friends were cheering!

And suddenly he felt
a little bit more determined ...

. . . to have another try.

So, he picked himself up and in he went . . .

again.

And again.

And again.

And after a LOT of agains . . .

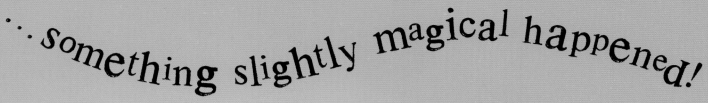

...something slightly magical happened!

Love Monster would like to have said that he surfed the extremely big wave. But the extremely big wave . . .

sort of surfed him.

And it was the
BEST. THING. EVER.

And although he might not have been
THE. BEST. SURFER. IN. THE. WORLD.
just yet ...

he was certainly the one who had
tried the most.

And, somehow, those waves just didn't seem
so extremely **big** any more.

You see, sometimes,
perfect is just …

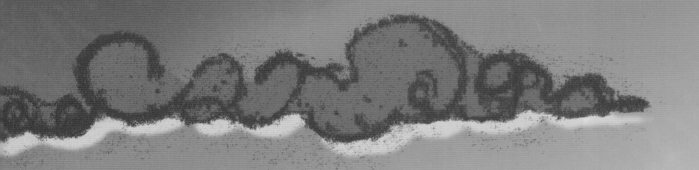

One more practice away.

To all the surfers
of this great wave we call life:
it's not how many times you wipe out that matters.
but how many times you get back on your board.

(& for my beautiful River & Sky . . . I know you will ride
every big wave that comes your way with strength & style.)
Also for Hattie (whose dad makes wonderful waves of colour in the world!)

First published in hardback and paperback in Great Britain by HarperCollins *Children's Books* in 2021

1 3 5 7 9 10 8 6 4 2

HB ISBN: 978–0–00–840832–9
PB ISBN: 978–0–00–840833–6

HarperCollins *Children's Books* is a division of HarperCollins*Publishers* Ltd.
1 London Bridge Street, London SE1 9GF • 1st Floor, Watermarque Building, Ringsend Road, Dublin 4, Ireland

Text and illustrations copyright © Rachel Bright 2021

The author/illustrator asserts the moral right to be identified as the author/illustrator of the work.
A CIP catalogue record for this book is available from the British Library.
All rights reserved.
No part of this publication may be reproduced, stored in a retrieval system or transmitted
in any form or by any means, electronic, mechanical, photocopying, recording or otherwise,
without the prior permission of HarperCollins*Publishers* Ltd.

Visit our website at: www.harpercollins.co.uk

Printed in Italy